LITTLE MAN THE TROLL

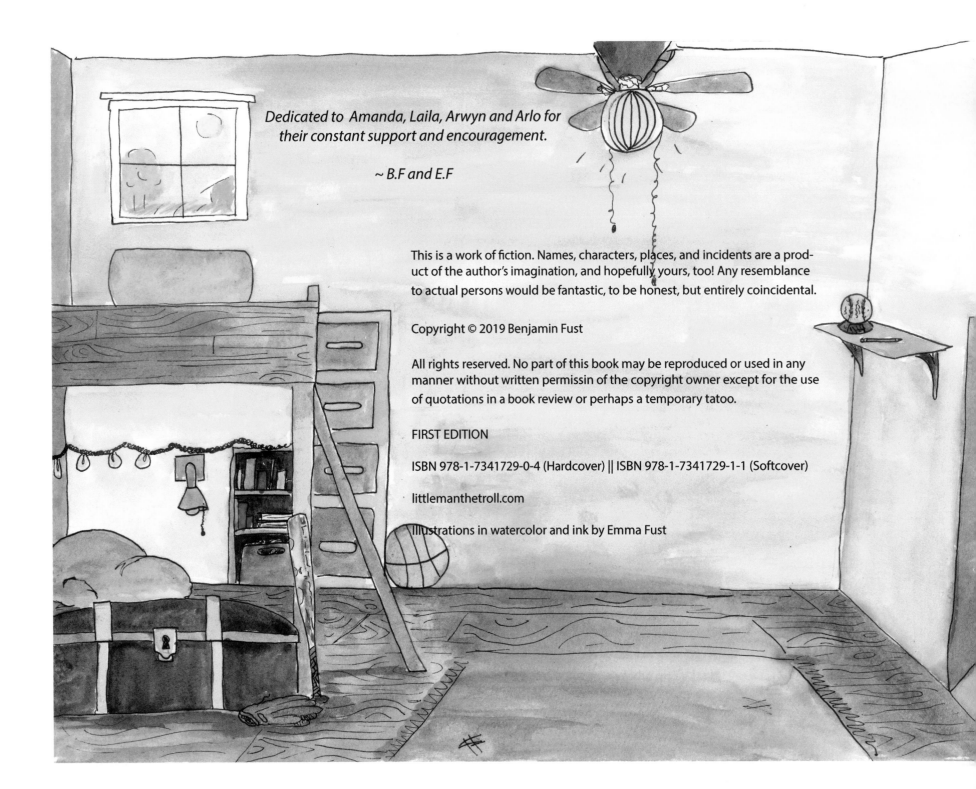

Dedicated to Amanda, Laila, Arwyn and Arlo for their constant support and encouragement.

~ B.F and E.F

FIRST EDITION

ISBN 978-1-7341729-0-4 (Hardcover) || ISBN 978-1-7341729-1-1 (Softcover)

littlemanthetroll.com

Illustrations in watercolor and ink by Emma Fust

LiTTLE
MAN
THE
TROLL

There's a sleepy tale about a troll
you may have never heard.
He lives above your eyelids and
has been there since your birth.

His name is Little Man the Troll

and there's one for every head.

He seldom stirs within the day

but awakes while you're in bed.

Have you noticed that your socks are off?

And your hair appears unkempt?

Crazy things that happened

in the night while you slept?

This is Little Man the Troll,

having all his fun.

Read ahead to take a peek

at all the things he does.

AHCHOOOOOO!

AHCHOO!

Right when you begin to sleep

and your eyelids start to close,

Little Man will tumble down

and itch your tired nose.

He'll tickle it with feathers

and crawl in on his knees,

but he's learned to be quite careful

in case you have to sneeze!

He'll jump into your ears and then climb into your head

to play some dreams for you to watch

while snoozing in your bed.

Sometimes he likes to frighten you

by showing scary dreams,

of ghosts at night,

and dogs that bite,

and other frightful things.

But then he shows the happy dreams

of candy canes and sun,

of rainbows, bikes, and kids you like,

and trolls, of course, for fun!

Sometimes he'll climb up to your head

and mess up all your hair.

He'll tug and pull and grab and push

and put it everywhere!

And why, you ask, would Little Man

stand your hair on end?

The answer's oh so clear to see,

it's so it looks like his!

When Little Man is hungry

he slides down to your mouth,

and roasts a couple hot dogs

on the hotness of your breath.

There's no way then to cool your mouth

when his cooking's done,

so he dumps water on your lips,

and that's where drool comes from!

And if you still don't think it's true

that nighttime trolls exist,

then think of how your belly button

gets all those balls of lint!

Of course you know it's Little Man, that's where he throws away,

all the fallen eyelashes he finds during the day.

Some people try to stay awake
or pretend like they're asleep,

to try and see their Little Man
as he does these sneaky things.

But he's quicker than the fastest eye

and smarter than you'd think.

He'll jump back to his hiding spot

if you even so much as blink.

Eventually the morning comes

and you slowly rise up to see,

that your hair's a mess and your lips are wet

and you really have to sneeze!

But sometimes you'll wake up sitting still,

your body hardly moved...

To Do List:
1.) Hide food from dogs
2.) Take nap
3.) Keep napping
4.) Feeling cute...buy new hat?
5.) Clean feather (eww!)

And wonder what happened to Little Man...

And guess,

that for just one night...

He must have been sleeping, too.

CPSIA information can be obtained at www.ICGtesting.com
Printed in the USA
LVIW011815171219
640673LV00009BA/67